Oliver Twist

RETOLD BY
MAGGIE PEARSON

ILLUSTRATED BY
NICK HARRIS

First published in 2011 by
Franklin Watts
338 Euston Road
London NW1 3BH

Franklin Watts Australia
Level 17/207 Kent Street
Sydney NSW 2000

Text © Franklin Watts 2011
Illustrations by Nick Harris, © Franklin Watts 2011
Cover design by Peter Scoulding

A CIP catalogue record for this book
is available from the British Library.

Picture acknowledgements:
Front cover: Tom Chiarolini/istockphoto: b. Alex Max/istockphoto: b/g.
p.46: Grafissimo/istockphoto

ISBN: 978 1 4451 0457 7

Dewey Classification: 823.9'14

3 5 7 9 10 8 6 4 2

Printed in Great Britain

Franklin Watts is a division of Hachette Children's Books,
an Hachette UK company.
www.hachette.co.uk

Contents

Chapter One: Orphan Oliver 5

Chapter Two: Meeting the Dodger 12

Chapter Three: Learning a trade 18

Chapter Four: A chance for Oliver 23

Chapter Five: Capture! 28

Chapter Six: A robbery goes wrong 34

Chapter Seven: A new start 39

Chapter One
Orphan Oliver

"That boy was born to be hanged!" roared the warden of the workhouse.

"What boy's that, Mr Bumble?" asked the matron.

"What boy? Oliver Twist, ma'am! That boy will dangle from the hangman's rope some day, or my name's not Bumble."

His name was Bumble.

But the boy's father's name wasn't Twist. And Oliver was not the name his mother would have chosen if she'd given him a name before she died giving birth to him in the workhouse.

Above all, this boy was not born to be hanged. He was born to be a hero.

"What's he done, Mr Bumble?" asked the matron. "What was his crime?"

"His crime? I hardly dare to tell you. At dinner today, he only asked for more!"

"Oh, Mr Bumble! He never did!"

Dinner in the workhouse that day and every day was a small bowl of gruel, which was like greasy washing- up water. It was horrible.

Who could possibly want more?

But growing boys get hungry.

The boys drew straws.

Oliver Twist was the unlucky winner.

That day at dinner Oliver finished his gruel, same as always. Licked his spoon clean and the bowl as well – so clean they never needed washing.

Then he took a deep breath, stood up, picked up his bowl and his spoon and started walking.

The dining room fell silent.

Every eye was on him.

Oliver could hear the sound of his own breath, the slip-slap of his bare feet on the cold stone floor. The beat of his heart was like thunder in his ears.

He stopped and looked up at Mr Bumble, still poised over his cauldron of gruel with the ladle in his hand.

"Please, sir," said Oliver, "may I have some more?"

Mr Bumble stared down at Oliver, thinking his ears must be playing tricks on him.

So Oliver said it again. "Please, sir, may I have some more?"

About what happened next, well let's just say that if the floor had opened up there and then and swallowed poor Oliver straight down to Hell, it would have been a mercy.

"That boy must go," declared Mr Bumble, "before he infects the rest!"

The very next morning a notice appeared on the workhouse gates:

BOY FOR SALE
£5
OR NEAR OFFER

In the end, Mr Bumble was happy to settle for three pounds from the undertaker, Mr Sowerberry.

So Oliver was cast out of the workhouse into the world of work. He was fed not on gruel, but on kitchen scraps even the dog had refused. He slept alone at night on the hard, cold floor among the coffins.

Worst of all was the undertaker's apprentice. "Born in the workhouse, was you?" he jeered. "That shows your ma was a wrong 'un! There's only one sort of woman ends up in the workhouse. You're lucky you weren't born in jail!"

It wasn't true. Oliver knew it wasn't true.
His mother was an angel in heaven,
watching over him.

"Not making a very good job of it, is she?"
sneered the apprentice.

Oliver had had enough.

He went for the apprentice – "Like a mad thing!" sobbed Mrs Sowerberry to Mr Bumble, when he was sent for.

"Have you been feeding him meat?" demanded Mr Bumble. "You should never feed them meat. Workhouse boys aren't used to meat. It drives 'em wild."

"Just take him away, Mr Bumble. Please!"

From inside the coffin where they had trapped him, Oliver heard every word. He knew it was now or never. The moment the coffin lid was lifted, Oliver was off.

Out of the door he fled and down the street and out of the town.

He ran and ran till he could run no more. After that he walked until he could walk no more. Then he lay down and slept.

When Oliver got up, he walked again, begging a crust of bread here and a cup of water there.

And so, in the end, he came to London town.

Chapter Two
Meeting the Dodger

London! Oh, London! It was so different from everything Oliver had ever known. The colours! The smells! The noise! Houses so tall they brushed the sky. People rushing hither and thither – buying and selling.

"Buy my sweet oranges!"

"Ripe strawberries, ripe!"

"Knives to grind!"

Oliver was dazzled, deafened, jostled and trodden on, shouted at, almost run over and spun round like a top.

Suddenly he felt a hand on his shoulder.

A voice in his ear said, "You new in town?"

It was a boy about his own age, but dressed in a man's suit of clothes and a top hat worn at a jaunty angle.

"Got somewhere to stay?" asked the boy.

Oliver shook his head.

"You hungry?"

Oliver nodded so hard it was a wonder his head didn't come clean off.

"Come on then."

The boy set off and Oliver followed, down ever more narrow, dark, shabby and smelly alleyways.

"They call me the Artful Dodger," the boy said over his shoulder. "Dodger for short."

"I'm Oliver," said Oliver. "Oliver Twist."

They came at last to a grimy front door.

"Here we are," said Dodger. "Home sweet home."

Up the rickety stairs they climbed, to a long attic room even more dark and dingy than the alley below.

But it was warm and filled with the smell of cooking.

"Who's there?" cried a voice.

"It's me, Fagin."

"Dodger?"

A man loomed out of the gloom. He wore a long, greasy coat. His hair, too, was long and greasy. He had a toasting fork in his hand with a sausage spiked on the end.

"Oliver," said Dodger. "Meet Fagin."

"Pleased to meet you, Oliver," said Fagin. "Have a sausage."

Oh, the taste of that sausage to a boy who'd been fed on gruel and kitchen scraps his whole life long!

"Have another!" said Fagin. "Before the rush starts."

From the alley below came the sound of running feet. Up the stairs they came, the door burst open and suddenly there were boys everywhere. Fat ones. Thin ones. Tall, short and middling. Fair, dark and ginger. They crowded round the table, calling for their dinner.

"Payment first," said Fagin. "Dinner afterwards."

He went round the table, collecting a handkerchief here, a watch there. One boy held out a wallet lined with banknotes.

"What do you think of that, Oliver?" said Fagin. "Isn't it fine?"

"It is, sir," said Oliver. "Very fine. Did he make it himself?"

Fagin laughed. "Would you like to learn a trade, Oliver, like my boys?"

"Oh, I would, sir!"

"Then come here and look at this here handkerchief. Can you see what's wrong with it? Those initials, Oliver! They'll have to be picked out with a pin. Do you think you could do that for me?"

"I'm sure I could, sir!"

"You're a good boy, Oliver. You'll do well."

After dinner, they all played a game. Fagin put some of the handkerchiefs in his pockets and walked up and down while two of the boys tried to steal them from his pockets without him noticing. There was lots of laughing and good-natured teasing as the boys threw themselves into the game. Oliver had never had so much fun before in his whole life.

Chapter Three
Learning a trade

The next day when Oliver woke up, the boys had all gone off to work. Oliver was left alone with Fagin, picking the stitches out of handkerchiefs.

In the evening the boys came back and they played the handkerchief game again. It was the same the next day and the next.

Now and then they had a visitor.

Sometimes it was a lady called Nancy. Her clothes were shabby and there was a sadness about her, but she had a smile that would warm the coldest heart.

Other times it was a man called Bill Sikes. You never saw Bill without his dog. The dog's name was Bullseye and they were two of a kind. Both squat, sour-tempered mongrels. Both wearing the scars of many a fight won and lost.

The boys kept their heads down while Bill was there. They stared at their plates, though no-one was eating. Fagin muttered, looked shifty and shook like a leaf long after Bill had taken his money and gone.

So the days passed. Oliver spent his time picking the initials out of handkerchiefs and wondering when he was going to start learning a trade.

Then one evening, after they'd played the handkerchief game and Oliver had done really well at it, the Dodger said, "I think he's ready, Fagin. Can I take him with me tomorrow?"

"Please, please, let me go!" begged Oliver.

"Just let me try him out," said the Dodger.

Fagin gave in. "All right, you can go. Keep out of trouble, Oliver. Bring him back safe, Dodger, you hear me?"

"I hear you," said Dodger.

There Oliver stood again, amongst the hustle and bustle of London.

Where was the Dodger? For a moment Oliver thought he'd lost him.

No! There he was, beside an old gentleman browsing outside a book shop. He was reaching under the gentleman's coat tails, as if he was playing the handkerchief game.

The Dodger turned and winked at him. In his hand was the gentleman's wallet.

This wasn't a game!

Oliver stood round-eyed as the Dodger fled past him.

"Come on, Oliver! Run!"

Oliver couldn't move.

"Stop! Thief!" cried the old gentleman.

The cry was soon taken up; "Stop thief! Stop that boy! Arrest him!"

Then Oliver ran.

But there was no sign of the Dodger and he was soon lost in a maze of twisting alleyways. On he ran, the thunder of feet on cobblestones echoing behind him. Hands reached out to clutch him. Feet tried to trip him up. A fist laid him flat on his back. There he was punched, kicked and spat on before being hauled up by his hair.

"Is this the boy?"

"No." The old gentleman shook his head. "This is not the boy who robbed me."

The crowd melted away.

"I'm so sorry," said the old man. He was staring at Oliver. "What is your name, boy?"

"Oliver, sir. Oliver Twist."

"Where do you live?"

"I don't know, sir."

"You don't know? Where are your parents?"

"They're dead, sir. I'm an orphan."

"I see. In that case, you'd better come home with me. My name is Mr Brownlow."

Chapter Four
A chance for Oliver

The next morning when Oliver woke, he
thought at first he had died and gone to
heaven. The bed was soft, the sheets were
clean and there was a scent of flowers in the
air. If, when the door opened, he'd seen the
mother he'd dreamed of standing there,
he wouldn't have been at all surprised.

Instead it was the housekeeper Mrs Bedwin
to say that breakfast was ready downstairs.
And if Oliver was afraid of being put back
out on the street, they'd have to carry him
over her dead body.

Back at Fagin's, the boys had waited in vain
for their dinner.

Now they waited in vain for breakfast while
Fagin went on fretting and fuming and

pacing up and down. Now and then he lashed out at the Dodger, but the Dodger was always too quick for him. He'd had years of practice.

"I told you to bring him back safe!" raged Fagin.

"What did you expect me to do?" said Dodger. "Carry him?"

"He'll lead the police straight to us."

"He won't," said Dodger. "He doesn't know the way."

"Good point! Good point!" Fagin nodded. "But he knows all our names. Our faces. Bill's too! Oh my godfathers! If Bill gets to hear of this I'm dead as mutton. What are we going to do, boys? We're none of us safe. All he's got to do is point the finger at one of us. Before you know it we'll hear footsteps on the stair and there'll come a knocking at that door –"

Knock! Knock!

Everybody froze.

It wasn't the police.

It was worse than that.

"Where is he?" roared Bill Sikes.

"Where's who, Bill?" said Fagin.

"You know who. Oliver Twist!"

"He's not here, Bill."

"I know that! I heard what happened. Get after him. Find out where he is. Then get him back, Fagin! Before he does for us all."

Back at Mr Brownlow's house, Mr Brownlow was telling his friend, Mr Grimwig, about Oliver.

"You've taken a street urchin into your home! What were you thinking of?" said Mr Grimwig.

"I was thinking," said Mr Brownlow, "of how much he reminded me of someone I used to know." His eyes strayed to the picture above the fireplace. It was a portrait of a young woman, who did look very much like Oliver.

"Sentimental rubbish!" said Mr Grimwig. "You know nothing at all about this boy."

"But I shall," said Mr Brownlow, "very soon. I've written to the workhouse where Oliver was born."

"A workhouse orphan?" said Mr Grimwig. "This gets worse. He's not to be trusted!"

"I do trust him," said Mr Brownlow.

He sent for Oliver.

"Oliver," he said. "Do you remember the bookseller's where we first met?"

"I do, sir!"

"Do you think you could find your way there?"

"I'm sure I could."

"Well, here's a parcel of books to take back. And a five pound note to pay for the ones I've decided to keep. There should be ten shillings change."

"That's the last you've seen of the boy, the books and the five pound note!" said Mr Grimwig. "Or I'll eat my hat!"

"You're wrong," said Mr Brownlow. "The boy will prove it."

Chapter Five
Capture!

Oliver trotted down the street, the books in his hand, a five pound note in his pocket and happiness in his heart.

"Oliver!" Someone was calling him.

"Oliver! Over here!"

"Nancy!" He ran to her arms.

Nancy hugged him as if she never meant to let him go. "Oliver, we've been so worried."

"I'm sorry, Nancy," said Oliver.

Before he could say any more, Bill Sikes had him in an iron grip.

"You wait till we get you home!" snarled Bill.

"Help me!" cried Oliver.

"He's my brother," Nancy told passersby.

"I'm not! I'm not!" Oliver struggled and kicked.

"He's always running off," said Nancy. "Little devil." She smiled.

The passers-by smiled back, nodded and strolled on.

So Oliver found himself back in Fagin's lair. The five pound note was safe in Bill's pocket. Fagin got the books and Oliver's nice new suit of clothes.

"Can I go now?" said Oliver. "Please let me go."

"Go where?" said Bill.

"Back to Mr Brownlow's."

"You can't go back there," said Fagin. "He thinks you're a thief."

"He doesn't!"

"You've taken his books, his money and the clothes he bought you."

"I didn't!"

"Are you going to tell him we took them?" said Bill.

"No!"

"Have you told him about us?" said Dodger.

"No!"

"I believe you," said Dodger. "Thousands wouldn't."

"What are we going to do with him then, Bill?" asked Fagin.

"Leave him to me!" said Bill.

Mr Brownlow didn't think Oliver was a thief. Long after Mr Grimwig had left (with a smug, told-you-so! look on his face) he sat waiting for Oliver to come home.

The next morning he planned to be off bright and early, to search for him. But first —

"We've got visitors. I put them in the drawing room," said Mrs Bedwin.

Mr Brownlow had written to the workhouse for information. He never expected the workhouse to come to him in the shape of Mr Bumble with the matron clinging to his arm. They were staring at the portrait above the mantelpiece.

"It's her, Mr Bumble!" whispered the matron. "Oh, Mr Bumble, what have we done?"

"What have you done?" demanded Mr Brownlow.

"Oh! Only kept it safe for the boy all these years, sir; I swear!" The matron held out a plain, gold locket.

Mr Brownlow took it and opened it. Inside were two locks of hair, one dark, one fair, and a wedding ring with the name Agnes engraved inside.

His eyes filled with tears.

"You kept it?" he said.

"All these years, sir. I was just keeping it safe for the boy."

"You stole it!"

"Ooh! I never did!"

"These things," said Mr Brownlow, "would have helped you to find her friends, her family. All you had to do was put an advertisement in the newspapers."

"That would have cost money, sir," said Mr Bumble. "And speaking of money, your letter did say something about a reward…"

"A reward?" said Mr Brownlow. "You stole the lady's locket and wedding ring and starved her child half to death. Get out before I call the police!"

"Oh, poor Agnes!" he sighed after they'd gone. "Poor Oliver!"

But where was Oliver?

Chapter Six
A robbery goes wrong

"Don't do this, Bill!" Nancy begged. "If Oliver says he won't tell on us, he won't."

"I'm going to make sure he won't," said Bill. "There's this house I've had my eye on. Oliver's going to get me inside."

"You're going to turn him into a thief!"

"That's right. Then if he turns us in, he'll go to jail along with the rest of us. Come on, Oliver."

Nancy watched them go. "I won't let you do it, Bill Sikes!" she whispered. "I won't let you turn him into a thief."

Mr Brownlow had searched for Oliver all day. Now he was sitting down to his dinner, though he'd got no appetite for it, when there came a frantic knocking at the door.

Mrs Bedlow went to open it.

"Is this Mr Brownlow's house?" said Nancy.

"It is."

"Tell him if he wants to see Oliver Twist again to come to London Bridge at midnight tonight."

"Come in and tell him yourself," said Mrs Bedlow kindly. "Rest for a while."

"I mustn't," said Nancy. "I daren't. I've been gone too long already. Just tell him to be there."

And she was gone.

"I can't do this, Bill," said Oliver.

"You can," said Bill Sikes. "And you will."

They were standing outside a big, rambling house, looking up at a tiny window.

"In you go," said Bill, lifting him up and in through the window.

Oliver found himself in a tiny cloakroom.
To the left he could see the front door.

"I won't be a thief!" thought Oliver.

"You get that front door open," said Bill,
"and let me in. Don't make a noise. I've got
a gun and I'll use it on you, if I have to!"

But before Oliver could take a step, Bill
accidentally fired his gun.

The noise was deafening.

Oliver wasn't hurt, but the noise made him dizzy. He tumbled backwards. Bill caught hold of him and hauled him back through the window.

"Come on," said Bill. "Run!"

Upstairs, lights were being lit and windows flung open. Oliver could hear people shouting and dogs barking as Bill half dragged, half carried him away.

Bill was in a terrible rage by the time they got back to Fagin's lair.

"Oliver's useless, Fagin! He's worse than useless! He'll get the lot of us hanged!"

He looked around suspiciously. "Where's Nancy?"

"I'm here, Bill," said Nancy, taking off her shawl, still trying to get her breath back from running halfway across town. "Let me get you a drink. You want one, Fagin?"

Oliver crouched in a corner of the dingy room, shivering.

"Slip out when you can, Oliver," whispered Nancy. "Wait for me downstairs."

Before Oliver could ask her why, she'd slipped away.

Nancy was the life and soul of the party that evening; singing, laughing, pouring drinks and more drinks for Bill and Fagin. Then, as the church clocks struck half past eleven, she picked up her shawl and said,

"I'm off home now, Bill. You coming?"

"I'll come when I'm good and ready," he snarled.

"I'll see you later then."

It was a while before anyone noticed Oliver was missing.

"Get after him!" roared Bill.

Chapter Seven
A new start

Nancy's heart was beating fast as she hurried Oliver towards London Bridge.

What if the old gentleman didn't come? It was a hard thing she'd asked him to do. She might have been setting him up for a robbery – murder, even. What if he didn't come alone? What if he brought the police with him? What would she do then?

But no; there he was. That must be him.

He was turning towards them, holding out his arms to Oliver who was running towards him.

"Come with us, Nancy," said Oliver.

"Come with us," said Mr Brownlow. "You can start a new life."

"I can't," said Nancy. "Not without him. He'd never come and I can't leave him. You know who I mean, Oliver."

"I know," said Oliver. "I won't tell."

"I know you won't, Oliver." She turned away and was lost in the river mist and the darkness.

Nancy hoped to get home before Bill did. But he was there, waiting for her.

"Where have you been?" he said.

"Nowhere," she said. "Walking."

"With Oliver? Where is he?"

"Back with his own kind. Honest people. You won't get near him again."

"You fool! He'll do for us all, Nancy!"

"He won't, Bill. He promised. He won't say a word."

Bill wasn't listening. He was angry and drunk and frightened. "You might as well have put a noose around my neck!"

"Never, Bill. I'd never do anything to hurt you!"

Those were the last words she ever spoke.

He raised a thick stick and brought it down with all his strength again and again. Afterwards he stood like a man slowly waking from a nightmare.

Then he ran from the house and stumbled away through the dark, lonely streets.

Already he could hear cries of "Murder!"

Other men might have lost themselves in a place the size of London. But Bill Sikes had a dog. Everyone knew Bullseye.

Bill tried to get rid of him.

"Here, Bullseye!" said Bill. "Good dog!"

Bullseye looked at the rope with the big stone tied to it, then at the river close by. He sidled off to a safe distance.

But when Bill gave up and slouched away, the dog followed him.

It wasn't long before the cry went up,
"There's Bullseye!"

The hunt was on. People poured out of
houses and shops and pubs, first in a
stream, then in a flood that filled the streets
and lanes and alleyways to overflowing.

At last they had Bill cornered in an old
warehouse. He barred the door and fled up
the stairs away from the baying crowd.

Up, up, up he went, to the very top.

The mob was battering at the door.

But here was an opening like a doorway, with a winch for lifting up goods from boats on the canal below. The canal was dry now, the boats long gone, but the rope was still there. Bill smiled. All he had to do was lower himself down and steal away.

Quick as he could, he tied a loop in the free end of the rope. He was slipping it over his head when something made him turn.

Whatever he saw made him take a step back.

He cried out one word – "Nancy!" Then he fell, with the rope snaking after him.

The mob agreed it was as neat a job as the hangman could have done when they found him dangling there.

Late as it was when they got home, Mr Brownlow took Oliver into the drawing room. He pointed up at the portrait above the fireplace.

"Her name was Agnes," said Mr Brownlow. "She was your mother, Oliver. She was engaged to be married to a very good friend of mine. Then he died suddenly. I tried so hard to find her! You should never have been born in the workhouse. I'll do my best to make it up to you."

"Welcome home, Oliver," said Mrs Bedwin. "Now it's long past your bedtime."

Charles Dickens (1812–1870)

Charles Dickens was born on 7 February 1812 in Portsmouth. His family moved to London when Dickens was three.

Dickens endured a difficult childhood, as his entire family, apart from him, was briefly imprisoned for bad debt. Young Charles worked in a shoe-blacking factory to support his family. The family was later reunited and Dickens went to school, but he never forgot the poverty and hardship of factory life and brought the lessons and insights he learned there to his writing.

Charles Dickens in 1870

Dickens went on to become a successful journalist and writer. He published his first novel, *The Pickwick Papers*, in 1837, and

Oliver Twist followed in 1838. Over the course of his lifetime, Dickens wrote around twenty novels and many more articles.

Dickens died on 9 June 1870. To the end, he wrote and campaigned for social reform. He is buried in Westminster Abbey, London.

Oliver Twist (1838)

Oliver Twist was first published in monthly instalments in a newspaper, so readers had a long wait in between to find out what had become of Oliver!

Like most of Dickens' novels, *Oliver Twist* has a social issue at its heart – the poor orphan children of 19th-century London, who turned to crime to survive. Among them, Oliver is a true hero who would rather be poor than steal. Oliver's goodness is rewarded in the end, just as Sikes' evil is ultimately punished.

Titles in the CLASSICS RETOLD series:

978 0 4451 0461 4
Ebook edition: 978 1 4451 0818 6

978 0 4451 0460 7
Ebook edition: 978 1 4451 0815 5

978 0 4451 0458 4
Ebook edition: 978 1 4451 0819 3

978 0 4451 0462 1
Ebook edition: 978 1 4451 0817 9

978 0 4451 0459 1
Ebook edition: 978 1 4451 0816 2

978 0 4451 0457 7
Ebook edition: 978 1 4451 0820 9